SMELLY BILL

Daniel Postgate

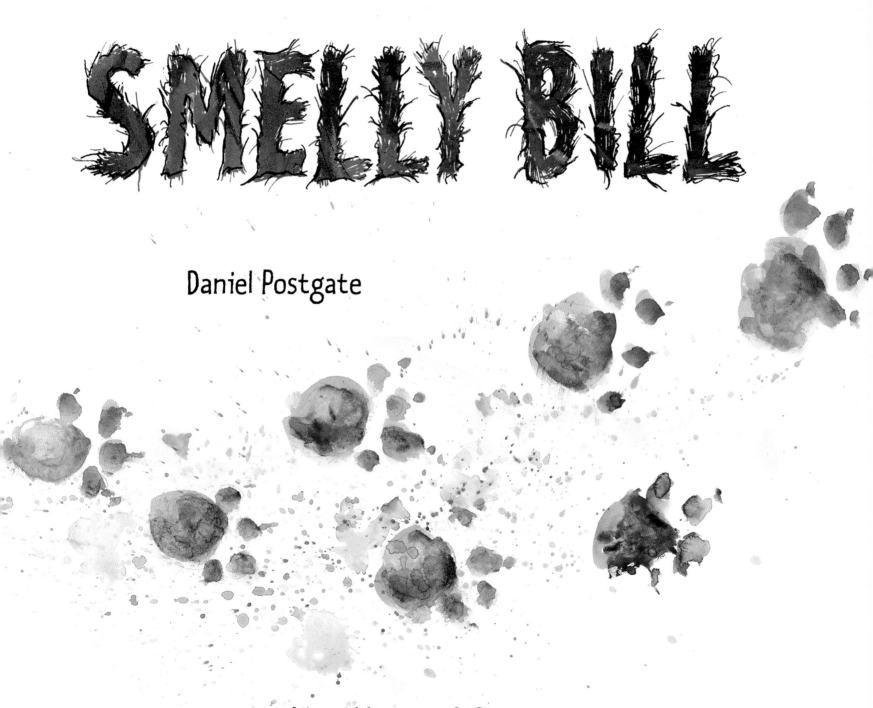

Albert Whitman & Company
Chicago, Illinois

Bill the dog loved smelly things,
Like muddy ponds and rubbish bins.
Disgusting stuff he'd stick his snout in,
Sniff and snort and roll about in.

Of course, because of this it meant
He had a most unpleasant scent.
His family would cry,

"You stink!"

And try to get him in the sink.

But every time he'd get away,
And live to stink another day.

A very smelly dog was Bill
And that's the way he stayed until...
One day his folks went to the beach

And left poor Bill **with**...

Great Aunt Bleach!

Now, Great Aunt Bleach just loved to clean.
On cleaning she was super keen.
With disinfectant, bucket, scrubber,
Vacuum, mop, and gloves of rubber,
Great Aunt Bleach yelled,

"Tally-ho!"

And cleaned the house from tip to toe.

When every knife and fork was polished,
Every dirty mark abolished,
Great Aunt Bleach said,

"What's that smell?"

And that is when she spotted Bill.

Bleach twittered,
"Come on, doggie-woo,
It's **bathie-wathie**
time for you!"

Bleach was fast, but Bill was faster.
Like a flash he dashed straight past her.
He knew exactly what to go for.

He scrambled underneath the sofa.

Just out of reach from Bleach he knew
That there was nothing she could do.
He snuggled up, that sassy chap,
And settled down to take a nap.

When Bill woke up, before his eyes
He saw a steak of mammoth size.
It was a lovely juicy thing.

It got him all a-dribbling.

Bill slid from underneath the seat
And sank his teeth into the meat.

It was a trick!

Bill had been fooled!

Bleach wound
and pulled
and wound
and pulled,

Until she had the smelly pet
Caught within her fishing net.

Then, with a laugh, Bleach filled the bath
Until the tub was brimming.
And while she tipped in smelly stuff,
Bill heard Great Aunty singing:

"Oh, fizzy, lilac-scented soaps,
Please hear the words I'm speaking;
Oh, apple blossom, lemon zest,
Cherry scrub, and all the rest,
Please do your very smelly best
To stop this beast from reeking."

While Bleach was mixing up her potion,
Bill struggled from the net.
And in one brisk and nimble motion,
Out the window leapt.

Across the yard he had to race
To find the perfect hiding place.
He dug down deep, down deep within
A very smelly compost bin.

But oh, **too late!**
Bleach spotted him.

She yelled, "You will not get away!"
And like a great plump bird of prey,
She swooped down to the compost bin...

And landed right on top of him!

"Game over, doggie-woggie-woo.
It's **bathie-wathie** time for you!"

When they returned, the family
Was most surprised and pleased to see
A fluffy Bill, from nose to toes,
Smelling sweeter than a rose.

Bleach said,
"I do not like to boast,
But I'm the one
to thank."

The children didn't get too close—
She absolutely stank!

For everyone at
Whitstable Day Nursery

The CIP record is available from the Library of Congress.

Text and illustrations copyright © 2005 Daniel Postgate.
First published in Great Britain by Meadowside Children's Books.
First published in the U.S. by North-South Books.
Published in 2010 by Albert Whitman & Company.
ISBN 978-0-8075-7463-8
Printed in China.
10 9 8 7 6 5 4 3 2 BP 15 14 13 12 11

For more information about Albert Whitman & Company,
please visit our web site at www.albertwhitman.com.